Copyright© 2022 Serenity Life Fitness Inc.

All rights reserved. No part of this book may be reproduced or used in any manner without the prior written permission of the copyright owner, except for the use of brief quotations in a book review.

To request permissions, contact the publisher at owners@serenitylifefitness.com .

First paperback edition February 2022

Cover art by Endy Astiko
Layout by Endy Astiko

Serenity Life Fitness Inc.
6615 Grand Avenue
#1009
Gurnee, IL 60099

This book is for my beautiful family who continues to show that despite our challenges, we have GRIT!

It's a typical Saturday morning in Tyler's home. The house is full of activity, noise, and delightful smells from the kitchen. "Good morning, Tyler," his mom says as she flips over the fluffy pancakes for breakfast. Tyler could smell the yummy chicken sausages sizzling in the skillet next to the pancakes. "Good morning, mom," he says with hunger in his eyes. "I'm guessing you want the usual- pancakes and sausages for breakfast," she says. Tyler nodded his head with a big smile on his face as he darted over to pick up his iPad. Tyler loves Saturdays. Saturdays mean no school, pancakes for breakfast, and lots of extra game time!

"Tyler before you get on that game of yours, I need you to read me a story," says his mom. "Oh mom, really? Do I have to?" groaned Tyler. "Reading is hard, and I just want to play my game."

"Well, I know that reading is hard, but you have to keep trying," says his mom. "It may not come easy to you honey, but you have to have GRIT. You just keep trying your best and never give up. One day, you will be reading big books with even bigger words." Tyler frowns and squenches his eyes, "Mom, what's GRIT?"

Mom slaps two pancakes and three sausages on his plate and says, "Well, it's like when you were learning to ride your bike without training wheels, and you kept falling. You didn't give up now did you? You kept trying because you were determined to ride that bike. You showed Dad and I that you had GRIT. It takes GRIT to be mentally fit. Do you get it now?" "Um, I guess, kind of," says Tyler.

Just then, Taj runs into the kitchen with his cars. He plops himself down on the floor and starts to play. "AHHHHHHHHH booom!" Taj screams as he mimics the sounds cars make when they crash. "Mommmmyyyyyyy, I gotta go potty," Taj yells with his big brown eyes. "Okay," says his mother as she picks Taj up and runs him to the bathroom to put him on the toilet. Tyler begins to think, "Hmmmmm, maybe GRIT is what Taj shows while he is learning to use the bathroom on his own. He sometimes has accidents, but he doesn't give up on that potty training thing."

After breakfast, Tyler makes it his business to figure out what GRIT looks like in his family. He peeks out the window and sees his dad playing football with his older brother Mason. Every time Mason drops the ball instead of catching, his dad makes him stop and give him ten pushups. "Sheesh, that's tough," Tyler thinks to himself.

He notices that even though Mason struggles with his push-ups, HE DOESN'T GIVE UP. That looks like GRIT. I guess it takes GRIT to make your body fit.

BA BOOM BOOM BOOM, BA BOOM BOOM BOOM! "What is that loud noise?" Tyler asks himself. As he runs closer to Makenzie's room, he could hear the music get louder and louder. Tyler burst through the door without even knocking. "Uggggghhhhh get out Tyler! Why are you in my room?" screamed his sister, rolling her eyes. "Dang, why you have to be so mean? I just wanted to know what you were doing," replied Tyler. "If you must know, I'm practicing this dance I learned at cheer, now GET OUT!" she screamed.

As she shoves him out of her room, he could hear her start the song over and over again. Every time she would forget the choreography, she would have to start all over again. "I guess Makenzie is using GRIT to learn her dance for cheer," he thought.

BA BOOM BOOM BOOM!

Tyler decided he would make his way outside where his dad and Mason were. Mason and his dad were in the garage where all the heavy exercise machines were. Dad was teaching Mason how to use the machines. "Since you struggle with your pushups son, I need you to work on this machine to help you get stronger," said his dad. Mason did ten chest presses, smiled, and flexed his muscles. "Look at these guns, Tyler. You have to work for these," said Mason. "Stop the cap!" mocked Tyler as he walks away. His brother seemed to always exaggerate about his looks.

On his way back to the kitchen, Tyler couldn't help to notice that his mom was in her office.
"Mom, I'm gonna try to read that book again." he said. But she didn't hear him. She was focused on saying her affirmations. When he peeked in the office, he could see her sitting down on her mat with her legs crossed and eyes closed.

She was breathing slowly but heavy. He heard her saying, "My body is a tremendous gift, and I will treat it with love and kindness."

"Mom must say that stuff so she can get through all her workouts for the week. She teaches like a gazillion fitness classes, and I don't know how she does it," Tyler thought to himself.

Tyler finally finds his way back to the kitchen. On the table, he saw the book that his mom asked him to read. Even though he knew that the book would be tough, he suddenly felt like he could try. And so he did.

Later in the week, it was time for Tyler to go to basketball practice. During one of the basketball drills, Tyler slipped and fell on the gym floor. Other kids laughed at him, but he got up and continued the drills. He could see his family in his mind. "It takes GRIT to be the best basketball player I can be," he said.

The next day, Tyler was at school and didn't really want to eat the broccoli on his plate. He thought of his family in his mind, and thought he should try it anyhow. "I'm going to need to eat more veggies if I want to grow big muscles like my dad and Mason," he thought.

When his mom picked Tyler up for school that day, she asked him how his day went. "It was good," he said. "Oh really?" asked his mom. "So what did you learn today?" "Well mom, remember when you were trying to teach me what GRIT means? I finally get it now. I understand that having GRIT means that even when things get tough, I should continue to try. It also means working hard doesn't always feel good, but I can always feel proud of myself when I do my best. "I think you finally got it son!" exclaimed his mom with a pleased look on her face.

"Don't you ever forget that it takes GRIT to be fit." "I won't," remarked Tyler. "And I will try the book when we get home." "That's what I'm talking about," exclaimed his mom. "Keep going after everything your heart desires, and NEVER EVER GIVE UP!" Tyler smiled. He knew that he had his family to always think of when things got tough. He decided from that point on, he would always use GRIT, especially when he wanted to quit.

Author Page

Natoia Franklin is an educator, Holistic Health Coach, personal trainer, and group fitness extraordinaire for women and children. As the owner of Serenity Life Fitness and co-founder of RHYTHM Academy, she offers services that inspire physical, mental, and spiritual transformation. She is passionate about serving underserved communities while ensuring that those communities get access and exposure to effective wellness programs that target obesity, poor nutrition, mental health issues, and sedentary lifestyles. When she is not training or teaching, she is busy being a mom to her four children and wife to her husband. Website: www.serenitylifefitness.com

Made in the USA
Middletown, DE
11 May 2022